HEDGEHOG HOWDEDO

Lynley Dodd

PUFFIN BOOKS

My garden's FULL of hedgehogs,
they're sleeping two by three,
under every flower,

every bush

and every tree.

There's one beneath the Pizza plant,

two are on a ledge,

I even saw three white ones
in a hole behind the hedge.

Four are on the compost heap,

five beside the shed

and six are sweetly snoozing
in the Cockleberry bed.

I'm sure I counted seven
in the Windywhistle grass

and eight are snoring loudly
in the woodpile,
bold as brass.

I can't think WHAT will happen
in just a month or two,
to the horde of hibernators
in this hedgehog howdedo.

I'm very glad it's winter,
it's such a lucky thing,

for there's going to be a traffic jam
when they wake up

in spring.

PUFFIN BOOKS

Published by the Penguin Group
Penguin Books Ltd, 80 Strand, London WC2R 0RL, England
Penguin Group (USA), Inc., 375 Hudson Street, New York, New York 10014, USA
Penguin Books Australia Ltd, 250 Camberwell Road, Camberwell, Victoria 3124, Australia
Penguin Books Canada Ltd, 10 Alcorn Avenue, Toronto, Ontario, Canada M4V 3B2
Penguin Books India (P) Ltd, 11 Community Centre, Panchsheel Park, New Delhi – 110 017, India
Penguin Group (NZ), cnr Airborne and Rosedale Roads, Albany, Auckland 1310, New Zealand
Penguin Books (South Africa) (Pty) Ltd, 24 Sturdee Avenue, Rosebank 2196, South Africa

Penguin Books Ltd, Registered Offices: 80 Strand, London WC2R 0RL, England

puffinbooks.com

First published by Mallinson Rendel Publishers Limited 2000
Published in Puffin Books 2002
9 10

Made and printed in Italy by Printer Trento Srl

British Library Cataloguing in Publication Data
A CIP catalogue record for this book is available from the British Library

ISBN-13: 978-0-14056-885-1